LITTLE GOLDEN BOOK® CLASSICS
Featuring the stories of
Margaret Wise Brown

Three Best-Loved Tales

MISTER DOG
Illustrated by Garth Williams

THE COLOR KITTENS
Illustrated by Alice and Martin Provensen

SEVEN LITTLE POSTMEN
By Margaret Wise Brown
and Edith Thacher Hurd
Illustrated by Tibor Gergely

A GOLDEN BOOK • NEW YORK
Western Publishing Company, Inc., Racine, Wisconsin 53404

MISTER DOG

The Dog Who Belonged To Himself

Illustrated by Garth Williams

Once upon a time there was a funny dog
named Crispin's Crispian. He was named
Crispin's Crispian because—

he belonged to himself.

In the mornings, he woke himself up and he went to the icebox and gave himself some bread and milk. He was a funny old dog. He liked strawberries.

Then he took himself for a walk. And he went wherever he wanted to go.

But one morning he didn't know where he wanted to go.

"Just walk and sooner or later you'll get somewhere," he said to himself.

Soon he came to a country where there were
lots of dogs. They barked at him and he barked
back. Then they all played together.

But he still wanted to go somewhere, so he
walked on until he came to a country where
there were lots of cats and rabbits.

The cats and rabbits jumped in the air
and ran. So Crispian jumped in the air and
ran after them.

He didn't catch them because he ran bang into a little boy.

"Who are you and who do you belong to?" asked the little boy.

"I am Crispin's Crispian and I belong to myself," said Crispian. "Who and what are you?"

"I am a boy," said the boy, "and I belong to myself."

"I am so glad," said Crispin's Crispian. "Come and live with me."

Then they went to a butcher shop—"to get his
poor dog a bone," Crispian said.

Now, since Crispin's Crispian belonged to himself, he gave himself the bone and trotted home with it.

And the boy's little boy bought a big lamb chop and a bright green vegetable and trotted home with Crispin's Crispian.

Crispin's Crispian lived in a two-story doghouse in a garden. And in his two-story doghouse, he had a little fur living room with a warm fire that crackled all winter and went out in the summer.

His house was always warm. His house had a chimney for the smoke to go out. And upstairs there was a little bedroom with a bed in it and a place for his leash and a pillow under which he hid his bones.

And there was plenty of room in his house for the boy to live there with him.

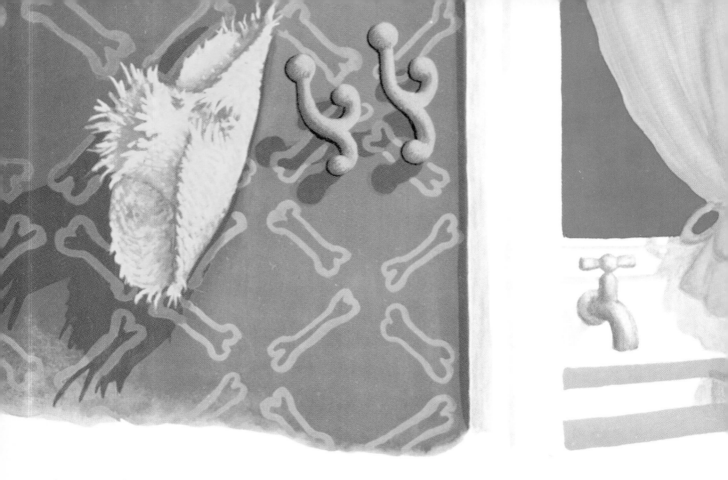

Crispian had a little kitchen upstairs in his two-story doghouse where he fixed himself a good dinner three times a day because he liked to eat. He liked steaks and chops and roast beef and chopped meat and raw eggs.

This evening he made a bone soup with lots of meat in it. He gave some to the boy, and the boy liked it. The boy didn't give Crispian his chop bone, but he put some of his bright green vegetable in the soup.

And what did Crispian do with his dinner?
Did he put it in his stomach?
Yes, indeed.
He chewed it up and swallowed it into his
little fat stomach.

And what did the little boy do with his dinner?
Did he put it in his stomach?
Yes, indeed.
He chewed it up and swallowed it into his
little fat stomach.

Crispin's Crispian was a *conservative.* He liked everything at the right time—
   dinner at dinnertime,
   lunch at lunchtime,
   breakfast in time for breakfast,
   and sunrise at sunrise,
   and sunset at sunset.
   And at bedtime—
At bedtime, he liked everything in its own place—
   the cup in the saucer,
   the chair under the table,
   the stars in the heavens,
   the moon in the sky,
   and himself in his own little bed.

And then what did he do?

Then he curled in a warm little heap and went to sleep. And he dreamed his own dreams.

That was what the dog who belonged to himself did.

And what did the little boy who belonged to himself do?
The boy who belonged to himself curled in a
warm little heap and went to sleep. And he
dreamed his own dreams.
That was what the boy who belonged to himself did.

GOOD NIGHT
AND
SWEET DREAMS.

THE COLOR KITTENS

Illustrated by Alice and Martin Provensen

Once there were two color kittens with green eyes, Brush and Hush. They liked to mix and make colors by splashing one color into another.

They had buckets and buckets of color
to splash around with. Out of these colors
they would make all the colors in the world.

The buckets had the colors written on them, but, of course, the kittens couldn't read. They had to tell by the colors. "It is very easy," said Brush.

"Red is red. Blue is blue," said Hush.

But they had no green. "No green paint!" said
Brush and Hush. And they wanted green paint, of
course, because nearly every place they liked to
go was green.

Green as cats' eyes
Green as grass
By streams of water
Green as glass.

So they tried to make
some green paint.

Brush mixed red paint and white paint together—and what did that make? It didn't make green.

But it made pink.

Pink as pigs

Pink as toes

Pink as a rose
Or a baby's nose.

Then Hush mixed yellow and red together,
and it made orange.

Orange as an orange tree

Orange as a bumblebee

Orange as the setting sun
Sinking slowly in the sea.

The kittens were delighted, but it didn't
make green.

Then they mixed red and blue together—and what did that make? It didn't make green. It made a deep dark purple.

Purple as violets

Purple as plums

Purple as shadows
On late afternoons.

Still no green! And then ...

O wonderful kittens! O Brush! O Hush!

At last, almost by accident, the kittens poured a bucket of blue and a bucket of yellow together, and it came to pass that they made a green as green as grass.

Green as green leaves on a tree

Green as islands in the sea.

The little kittens were so happy with all
the colors they had made that they began
to paint everything around them.
They painted ...

Green leaves
　　and red berries
and purple flowers
　　and pink cherries
Red tables
　　and yellow chairs
Black trees
　　with golden pears.

And by then, it was evening and the colors
began to disappear in the warm dark night.

The kittens fell asleep in the warm dark night
with all their colors out of sight, and as they slept
they dreamed their dream—

A wonderful dream
Of a red rose tree
That turned all white
When you counted three.

One... Two...

Three

And they dreamed that
A green cat danced
With a little pink dog

Till they all disappeared in a soft gray fog.

And suddenly Brush woke up and Hush woke up. It was morning. They crawled out of bed into a big bright world. The sky was wild with sunshine.

The kittens were wild with purring and pouncing—

Pounce

Pounce

Pounce

They got so pouncy, they knocked over the
buckets and all the colors ran out together.

There were all the colors in the world and
the color kittens had made them.

FIRST CLASS

INSURED

VIA AIR MAIL

VIA AIR MAIL

AIR MAIL
6¢
U.S. POSTAGE

SEVEN
LITTLE
POSTMEN

FRAGILE

CONTENTS — MERCHANDISE
POSTMASTER — THIS PARCEL
MAY BE OPENED FOR POSTAL
INSPECTION IF NECESSARY.
RETURN POSTAGE GUARANTEED.

Illustrated by
Tibor Gergely

SPECIAL DELIVERY

A boy had a secret. It was a surprise.
He wanted to tell his grandmother.
So he sent his secret through the mail.
The story of that letter
Is the reason for this tale
Of the seven little postmen who carried the mail.

Because there was a secret in the letter
The boy sealed it with red sealing wax.
If anyone broke the seal,
The secret would be out.

He slipped the letter into the mailbox.

The first little postman
Took it from the box,
Put it in his bag,
And walked seventeen blocks
To a big Post Office
All built of rocks.

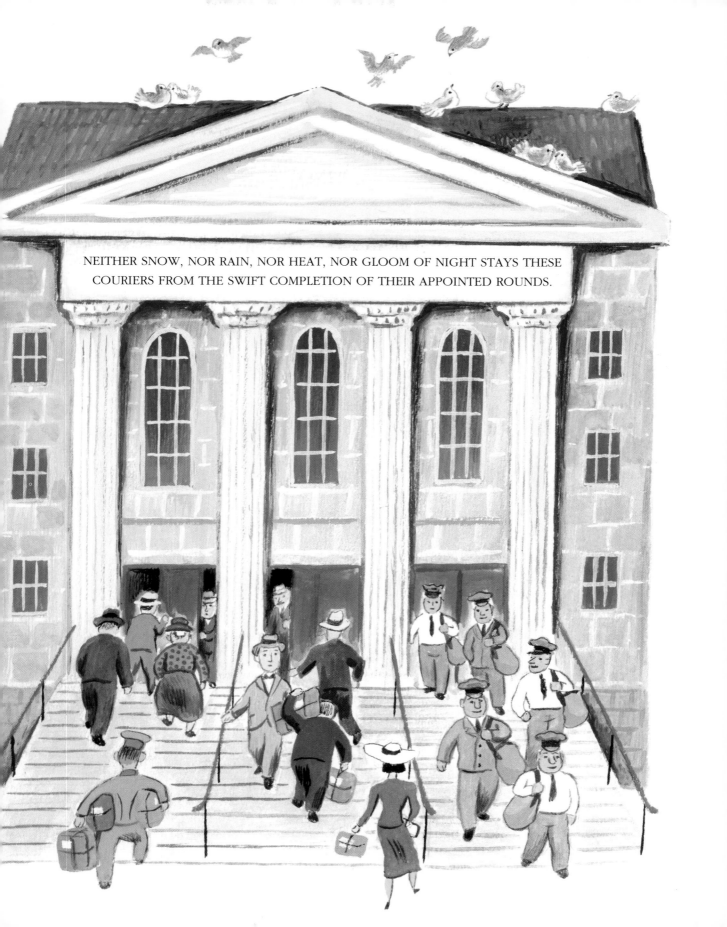

The letter with the secret
Was dumped on a table
With big and small letters
That all needed the label
Of the big Post Office.

Stamp stamp, clickety-click,
The machinery ran with a quick sharp tick.
The letter with the secret is stamped at last
And the round black circle tells that it passed
Through the canceling machine
    Whizz   whizz   fast!

Big letters
Small letters
Thin and tall—
The second little postman
Sorts them all.
The letters are sorted
From East to West
From North to South.

"And this letter
Had best go West,"
Said the second
Little postman,
Scratching his chest.
Into the pouch
Lock it tight
The secret letter
Must travel all night.

The third little postman in the big mail car
Comes to a crossroad where waiting are
A green, a yellow, and a purple car.
They all stop there. There is nothing to say.
The mail truck has the right of way!
"The mail must go through!"

Up and away through sleet and hail
This airplane carries the fastest mail.
The pilot flies through whirling snow
As far and as fast as the plane can go.

And he drops the mail for the evening train.
Now hang the pouch on the big hook crane!

The engine speeds up the shining rails
And the fourth little postman
Grabs the mail with a giant hook.

The train roars on
With a puff and a snort
And the fourth little postman
Begins to sort.

The train carries the letter
Through gloom of night
In a mail car filled with electric light

To a country postman
By a country road
Where the fifth little postman
Is waiting for his load.

The mail clerk
Heaves the mail pouch
With all his might
To the fifth little postman
Who grabs it tight.

Then off he goes
Along the lane
And over the hill
Until
He comes to a little town
That is very small—
So very small
The Post Office there
Is hardly one at all.

The sixth little postman
In great big boots
Sorts the letters
For their various routes—
Some down the river,
Some over the hill.

But the secret letter
Goes farther still.

The seventh little postman on R.F.D.
Carries letters and papers, chickens and fruit
To the people who live along his route.

He stops to deliver some sugar
To Mr. Jones, who keeps a store
And always seems to need something more.

For Mrs. O'Finnigan with all her ills
He brings a bottle of bright pink pills.

There were parts
For a tractor

And a wig for an actor.

There were dozens of chickens
For Mrs. Pickens

And a dress for a party
For Mrs. McCarty.

At the last house along the way sat the grandmother of the boy who had sent the letter with the secret in it. She had been wishing all day he would come to visit. For she lived all alone in a tiny house and sometimes felt quite lonely.

The postman blew his whistle and gave her the letter with the red sealing wax on it—the secret letter!

"Sakes alive! What is it about?"
Sakes alive! The secret is out!
What does it say?

THAT I'M COMING TO VISIT ON SATURDAY.
MY CAT HAS SEVEN KITTENS AND I AM BRINGING
ONE TO YOU FOR YOUR VERY OWN KITTEN.
THE POSTMAN IS #MY FRIEND.
                    YOUR GRANDSON
                        THOMAS

Seven Little Postmen

Seven Little Postmen carried the mail
Through Rain and Snow and Wind and Hail
Through Snow and Rain and Gloom of Night

Seven Little Postmen
Out of sight.
Over Land and Sea
Through Air and Light
Through Snow and Rain
And Gloom of Night—
Put a stamp on your letter
And seal it tight.

About
Margaret Wise Brown

Once called "laureate of the nursery," Margaret Wise Brown (1910-1952) spent much of her childhood in the woods on Long Island, chasing dragonflies and climbing cherry trees. Though she had few childhood companions, she acquired a menagerie of pets that included, by her own accounting: "one dog, thirty-six rabbits, a cat, a squirrel that bit me, seven goldfish, and two long-haired Peruvian guinea pigs."

After attending school in Switzerland, Margaret completed her B.A at Hollins College in Virginia. Upon her return to New York, she joined an experimental writing group at the Bank Street School. There she was urged to combine her talents as poet and storyteller to create children's books.

The first of these was *When the Wind Blew,* a fantasy based on a story by Chekhov and published in 1937 by Harper Brothers. Other lyrically simple, spellbinding children's books followed, among them the classic *Goodnight Moon* and *The Runaway Bunny,* also for Harper Brothers, and her many much-loved Little Golden Books. The hero of Mister Dog, included in this volume, is a canine known as Crispin's Crispian, named after one of Brown's most cherished pets.

The author had a brilliant sense of how to capture a child's attention. She found picture books to be a fascinating field and still relatively unexplored because, as she put it, "No one dares to be simple enough."

Only Margaret Wise Brown dared to write down the big noise of a fire engine in one of her books, for example, and then quietly tell children to listen to the sound of the sun shining. Only this author dared to toss in ten-dollar words like "ruminate" and "rapscallion," shocking the educators committed to the safe word lists of the day. The author was prolific and endlessly gifted.

In 1947, noted artist Leonard Weisgard received the prestigious Caldecott Medal for his illustrations for *The Little Island,* published by Doubleday. Happily, the text was written by Margaret Wise Brown. In 1984, after the author's death, the important Kerlan Award was given in honor of her life's work.